Reaching *for the* Sun

Story by Lisa Markowski
Illustrations by Berne Williams

Published by The de Sales Group, LLC

Text: Lisa Markowski
Illustrations: Berne Williams
Cover & Book Design: Harrah Lord

ISBN: 978-0-578-02653-4

Library of Congress Control Number to come

Printed in China

My Storytime Friends™ is an imprint of The de Sales Group, LLC

FIRST EDITION

2008 CPSIA tracking label:

Everbest Printing Co.
334 Huanshi Rd. South
Dachong Western Industrial District
511458 Nansha, Panyu, GUANDONG
Peoples Republic of China

Date of Production: August 1, 2009

Cohort: Batch 1

All the snow had melted in Bear Corners, New England. Trees were green and full, and flowers were sprouting everywhere.

Lanie Bear loved to smell the flowers as she walked to her grandparents' house. Grandma had a big rose garden that was Lanie's favorite place to be.

Although Lanie loved the pretty smell of the roses, she did not love the thorns. Ouch! She wanted to grow flowers, too, but ones without thorns would be better.

The first thing Lanie saw every morning was
a tall sunflower. It belonged to Mr. Harrington
next door, and it reached over the fence. Lanie
liked to watch the flower turn its face toward the sun.

How wonderful it would be if she could grow her own!

One day Mr. Harrington noticed Lanie admiring his sunflower. "I can see you really like that sunflower, Lanie," he said.

Lanie smiled. "Yes, Mr. Harrington! I sure do! Someday I want to grow sunflowers as tall as yours!"

Mr. Harrington smiled and set down his rake.

"Well, why not right now?
I have a packet of seeds here in my pocket."

Lanie's eyes grew wide—almost as wide as the happy face of the sunflower.

Mr. Harrington set a seed in Lanie's hand and told her how to plant it.

"Find the sunniest spot, and scratch a little dirt away with your paw," he explained. "Put the seed in, cover it with soil, and pat it. Then water it and watch for the little seedling to break through."

Lanie skipped happily around her yard until she found the perfect spot. She'd be able to see the flower from her room, and every bear  in Bear Corners would see it, too, as they passed by.

Lanie heard Mr. Harrington's voice in her
mind as she planted the seed.

MY
Sunflower

"Find the sunniest spot. Scratch some dirt away.
Put the seed in. Pat down the soil. Water it,
and watch for the seedling!"

Before she could
even say,
"Grow tall, little
sunflower,"
Lanie was done.
She sat on the grass
and waited for
the seed to
sprout.

But nothing happened.

"Lanie, dear," Mama called from the window. "It's time for lunch!" But Lanie did not want to miss the moment when her seedling poked through the soil.

"Mama," she answered. "May I eat my sandwich outside today?"

MY Sunflower

Lanie brought a lawn chair to the spot
where she'd planted the seed. She sat down
with her lunch and watched the ground closely,
waiting for the little, green seedling.
But still nothing happened.

The next day, Lanie ate breakfast, lunch,
& dinner in her lawn chair next to her seed.

But it didn't sprout.

She did the
same thing the next
day and the day after that,
until two whole weeks had gone
by with no sprout!

"Oh, Mama! I don't know what's wrong with my sunflower seed!" Lanie cried. "It just won't grow!" Mama hugged Lanie and said, "Don't worry, sweetheart. Mother Nature takes her time, and you just have to be patient."

But Lanie found it hard to be patient, especially as Mr. Harrington's sunflower grew taller and taller, until it made a shadow across Lanie's yard.

A shadow . . . a shadow! That's it!

Lanie jumped up from her chair. "Mr. Harrington! Mr. Harrington!" she called over the fence. Her neighbor looked up from his weeding and went over to see why Lanie was so excited.

"What does a sunflower need more than anything?" she asked.
"Well, I know the answer, because it's right in the name:

SUN!"

Lanie moved her chair away from the spot. "I've been sitting here so much that I blocked all the sun!"

Lanie smiled widely as she sat back down, no longer block-
ing the rays of sun her seed needed to sprout. In no time,
a little bit of green broke through the soil.

"It's here! It's here!" Lanie shouted. "My sunflower has finally sprouted!" That day she ate her lunch and dinner beside her seedling, but it had grown so big that she realized it didn't need her to watch over it all the time.

Lanie watered her seedling
once a day, and she couldn't
believe how quickly it grew.
Soon it was almost as tall as Mr.
Harrington's sunflower.
And then it grew
even taller!

Mama and Papa were so proud of Lanie, but not just because she had grown the tallest sunflower in Bear Corners. They were proud of her most of all because she had tried hard and she had never given up.

They were especially proud when Lanie grew up to be a sunflower farmer. She had the biggest sunflower farm anywhere in New England, and some of her sunflowers grew as high as the clouds!

All day long the flowers turned their faces toward the sun as they looked out over all of Bear Corners.